Tara Binns
Eagle-Eyed Pilot

by Lisa Rajan
Fenika Omiyale

When Tara Binns runs widdershins
Around the costume box,
The attic spins, the fun begins,
The magic clasp unlocks.

"Widdershins?
What's widdershins?"
Both you and Tara say,
It's when you run in circles
But go round the other way.

The box has big ideas,
And lots of hats and shoes,
It puts her in a costume
She wouldn't normally choose.

Each outfit brings adventure,
And takes her far away,
She shuts her eyes and wonders
"What will I be today?"

She's flying in a jumbo jet
At 30,000 feet,
A smart peaked cap upon her head,
She's in the pilot's seat.

They're cruising on the jet stream,
With darkening clouds in sight,
The deep blue sea is to the left,
And mountains to the right.

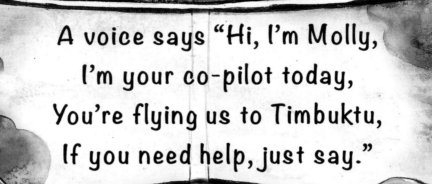

A voice says "Hi, I'm Molly,
I'm your co-pilot today,
You're flying us to Timbuktu,
If you need help, just say."

Tara viewed the dashboard
And said "Questions? I have two:
What are all the dials for?
And what do the buttons do?"

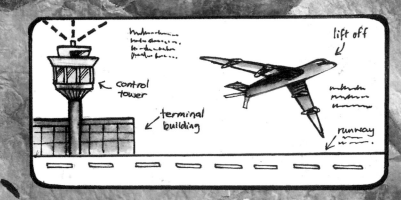

TIMBUKTU

ATLANTIC
OCEAN

EUROPE

AFRICA

Molly gave a lesson
In how planes climbed and turned,
And how to cruise, descend and land
And pretty soon, she'd learned.

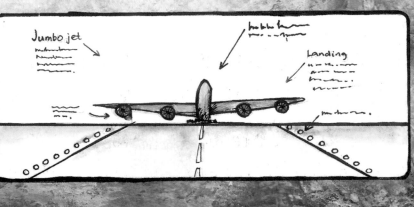

Then bright light filled the cockpit,
The lightning forked and flashed,
A storm was fast approaching,
And the rumbling thunder crashed.

The winds were getting stronger,
They lashed an island town,
Uprooting trees and bushes,
And blowing houses down.

Tara needed help so
She asked Molly and the crew,
"How do you deal with storms and
What would other pilots do?"

"Try to fly above it?
Take the plane straight through?
Steer the plane around it?
Yes – I think that's what I'll do."

"It's a very tough decision,
I can see why you are torn,
But most pilots fly above it,
They don't go around a storm."

"I'm going to go around it,
Like I did around the chest",
And she set the plane's coordinates
On a bearing heading west.

The storm clouds were avoided,
And they headed out to sea,
The flight was smooth and steady,
And the storm a memory.

Tara looked below them,
Pushed back her pilot's cap,
The little island coming up,
Looked like a treasure map!

"I think I see a cross made
By the palm trees on the sand,
There could be buried treasure,
We should find a place to land."

"This tree is in the centre
of where X marks the spot,
And there's just one way to find out
If there's treasure here or not."

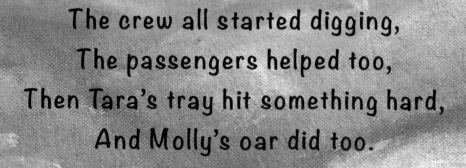

The crew all started digging,
The passengers helped too,
Then Tara's tray hit something hard,
And Molly's oar did too.

It was the biggest treasure chest
The girls had ever seen,
Full of gold and silver coins,
And jewels of red and green.

There were diamonds and sapphires,
And a cutlass made of gold,
And a jewel-encrusted crown,
From a treasure trove of old.

The pirates had buried it,
And then they'd sailed away,
And no one realised it was there
'Til Tara flew that way.

That night they had a party,
To celebrate their find,
But Tara sat there quietly,
With something on her mind.

"The storm has changed our fortunes,
For X did mark the spot,
We were very lucky, but
Some other folk were not."

"Many lost their homes today,
They must feel very bad,
I think that if we helped them,
I wouldn't feel so sad."

"Let's fly back to that island,
And use a parachute,
To send the treasure down to them,
Let's give them all the loot."

Molly beamed at Tara,
"What a brilliant idea!"
The passengers all clapped her,
And the crew all gave a cheer.

"You're a very special person,
And all of us can tell,
You're not just a great pilot,
You are super kind as well."

So dancing round the treasure chest,
Went happy Tara Binns,
And suddenly she'd realised –
She'd gone round widdershins.

The sand dunes started spinning,
She heard a loud KA-BOOM!!
And next thing she was back home
In that dusty attic room.

She took off the pilot's costume,
And the splendid captain's hat,
She thought of her adventure,
and sat down on the mat.

"Who knew that being a pilot
Could be such brilliant fun?
Next time I want a costume,
I'll pick that very one."

The chest replied "You kids should
Learn to fly and spread your wings,
The sky's the very limit,
You can do amazing things".

When Tara Binns
runs widdershins...

CAVENDISH ❊ KEBLE

Published by Cavendish Keble Ltd, 9 Perseverance Works,
Kingsland Road, London E2 8DD, UK.
All rights reserved.
First published in 2014 in the United Kingdom

A catalogue record for this book is
available from the British Library.

ISBN 978-0-9930082-0-7

For more copies of this book,
please email: info@cavendishkeble.com
Printed in China

she gets to do amazing things!

Tara Binns
Crash Test Genius

by Lisa Rajan
Eerika Omiyale

Coming soon...

In CRASH TEST GENIUS...
she becomes an engineer and a sudden accident gives her a brilliant idea that will make bumps, thumps, trips and falls a LOT more fun!

In DOUBLE CHOC DOC...
she becomes a doctor, and after seeing her patients suffer with coughs, colds and sneezes, Tara goes in search of a cure... and finds one in the unlikeliest of places.

Tara Binns
Double Choc Doc

by Lisa Rajan
Eerika Omiyale

Available from www.cavendishkeble.com

CAVENDISH ❋ KEBLE